Gunhilde and the Halloween Spell

written and illustrated by
VIRGINIA KAHL

CHARLES SCRIBNER'S SONS, NEW YORK

It was Halloween and the trees were bare;

There were ghosts and goblins everywhere.

Dark clouds scudded across the sky;

A giant owl hooted its eerie cry.

The flickering stars and the moon shone down

On a sturdy castle and nearby town.

In the castle, above the moat's dark waters,

Lived a Duchess, a Duke, and their thirteen daughters:

Madeleine, Gwendolyn, Jane and Clothilde,

Caroline, Genevieve, Maude and Mathilde,

Willibald, Guinevere, Joan and Brunhilde,

And the youngest of all was the baby, Gunhilde.

They were planning a night both exciting and merry,
With games that were fun and tales that were scary.

754847

"But first," said the Duchess, "we'll hurry on down
And join all the folk who have come from the town.
We'll watch as the villagers light up the fire
And throw on some faggots to make it burn higher."

They had dressed up as witches; in that attire
They wandered around to observe the fire.
For a fire made up of logs and switches
Is helpful in driving off ghosts and witches.

When Gunhilde grew cold, her mother said, "Please,
Wear this scarf to protect you against the breeze.
It's enough that your father is home in his bed
With sniffles that come from a cold in the head.
So remember, Gunhilde," the Duchess said brightly,
"To keep your new scarf wrapped around you tightly."
Then she warned them, "This night is a night to be wary,
For creatures are out that are evil and scary.
So, stay near me, girls. Don't wander away,
For bad things can happen to children who stray."

But the crowd was so restless, it pushed them along
And the girls wandered off,
        though intending no wrong.
They were jiggled and jostled
        and pushed up and down,
Till the eldest, Mathilde,
        exclaimed with a frown,

"We'd better go home now, before it's too late.
Let's look for our mother;
   come, don't make her wait."
But where she was standing,
   they hadn't a notion,
With so many people
   and so much commotion.

Then they spied a tall figure
      just leaving the crowd.
"There she goes—come on, girls!"
      cried Mathilde aloud.
They scrambled to catch her
      and hurried on after
With squeals and with whoops
      and a great deal of laughter.
Through brambles and thicket
      and into the wood
They hurried behind her
      as fast as they could.
But instead of going home
      as they all thought they should,
The figure went deeper,
      far into the wood.

The forest was inky;
      wind tore at their hats
Above and around them
      were hundreds of bats.
And no one observed,
      as they started to scramble,
That Gunhilde's scarf
      had been caught on a bramble.
So, the farther they went,
      why the more it unraveled.
It kept getting shorter
      the farther they traveled.
When they thought that they couldn't
      walk one footstep more,
They came to a hut
      with a broken-down door.

"Come in," said the figure that looked like their mother.
But when they stepped in, they saw it was another!
Another thin creature, one scrawny and tall—
It wasn't their mother, oh, no, not at all!

It wasn't their mother who shut the door tight;
It wasn't their mother who gave them a fright.

It wasn't the Duchess who waved a big switch.
No, it wasn't their mother—

it was a WITCH!

"Heh, heh, all my pretties,"
  she cackled in glee,
"you'll be in my power forever,
  you'll see."
She started to mutter;
  they heard her voice swell;
She waved a big switch
  and then uttered a spell:
"'Abbra-caddabra' and 'Pooh-pitti-pooh,'
I've cast an invincible spell over you.
And no one can guess
  (and I'll surely not tell)
The magical word
  that will break off my spell."

She had no sooner said this, when each little child
Turned into a toad, looking ugly and wild.
Thirteen small toads there were, bumpy and brown;
Thirteen small toads, jumping up and then down.
They had once been small girls who had happened to roam;
But now they were toads and they wished they were home.

Now, back at the fire, the Duchess stood nigh
And watched as the folk bade each other "Good-bye."
She waved to them all and then looked all around;
But there wasn't a trace of her girls to be found!
"Oh, where are my daughters?" she cried in despair.
"I can't find my children, no, not anywhere."
She rushed to the castle; the Duke was in bed.
"Our daughters are missing; come, find them," she said.
"I'm afraid," said the Duke, as he started to sneeze,
"That I shouldn't be out in the cold autumn breeze."
But the Duchess cried, "No, you can't go back to sleep.
Our children have vanished; I think I shall weep."

"There, there," said the Duke, "though the night is so dark,
We'll search through the castle and scour the park."

So they started to search—in the attic, the stables.
They looked behind cupboards and under the tables.
They went back to the fire and searched where they could,
And finally, they came to the edge of the wood.

And there, on a bramble, they spied a bright thread.
"Why, that's from Gunhilde's new muffler," they said.

"Let's see where it leads,"
        they both cried in delight.
"We'll find them and bring them
        home safely this night."

They followed the thread
        just as fast as they could,
Through brambles and thicket and
        on through the wood.
When they thought that they couldn't
        walk one footstep more,
They came to a hut
        and they knocked on
                the door.

When the door was thrown open,
      the Duke said, "My dear,
Our daughters are missing.
      We think they are here."
"I'm afraid," said the witch
      (for indeed it was she),
"You won't find them here."
      And she cackled in glee.
"For it's quite plain to see,
      if you look all around,
There are only a few
      dusty toads on the ground."

"Alas!" cried the Duchess
        and brushed back a tear,
"I was sure that we'd find
        all our children down here."
"All those toads," said the Duke.
        "It looks like a convention.
They're hopping around
        to attract our attention.
Well, our daughters aren't here.
        Now what shall we do?
And besides," said the Duke,
        "my cold is worse, too."

Just as the witch was beginning to gloat,

The Duke spied a toad with some wool round its throat.

The wool that they'd followed to this mean abode

Was tied round the neck of the tiniest toad!

With a pitiful croak and a hippity-hop

The little thing landed in front of him, "Plop!"

Then the Duchess looked down
     and exclaimed, "I declare,
That must be Gunhilde
     Who's hopping down there.
For she had a muffler
     of just that bright hue.
And now she's a toad.
     What *are* we to do?
Our girls are bewitched.
     Oh, alas and alack!
We'll never be able
     to get them all back."

The witch roared with laughter
  and stamped on the floor.
"You'll not see your girls again,
  not any more.
Toads they are now
  and toads they'll remain.
No, you'll not see your
  sweet little children again."

Then again the witch snorted and chortled in glee.
"There's a spell on your daughters as you plainly see.
I said 'Abbra-cadabbra' and 'Pooh-pitti-pooh';
Now they'll stay toads forever,
        not come back to you.

And you never can guess
        (and I'll surely not tell)
The magical word
        that will break off my spell."

They tried hundreds of words,
    all the ones they thought best;
But none broke the spell;
    no, not one that they guessed.

"Is it 'Zounds'?" asked the Duke,
    "or 'Diddle-dee-dee'?"

"Is it 'Quoof'?" asked the Duchess,
    "or is it 'Quee-Wee'?

Is it 'Presto'? 'Eureka'?
    or 'Fee-fie-fo-fum'?
Is it 'Skiddle-skeddaddle'
    or 'Dum-diddle-dum'?"

While they both kept on guessing,
the witch laughed, "Tee-hee.

Oh, you'll never guess
and won't get it from me!
You'll never find out
(and I'll surely not tell)
The magical word
that will break off my spell."

Whatever they tried,
didn't seem to be right.

"Go on," said the witch,
"you'll be guessing all night."

"I give up!" cried the Duchess
     and burst into tears.
"We'll never guess right
     in a million years."

Just then the Duke sniffled,
     "Oh, pardon me, please,
I've a terrible cold
     and I'm going to sneeze."

He took a deep breath,
     went "Ker-choo!" and then,

KER-

Went "Ker-choo!"
     and "Ker-choo!"
          and "Ker-choo!" again.
"Ker-choo!" he sneezed,
     and "Ker-choo!" once more.

CHOO

The witch jumped up and she stamped the floor.
"That's the word!" she shrieked wildly.
    "I said I'd not tell,
But you guessed and you've broken
        my magical spell."

At that very moment the toads became
Their missing daughters, the very same!
The toads had vanished without any traces
And thirteen girls had appeared in their places.

The Duke told the Duchess, "The first thing, my dear,
Is to carefully count them to see they're all here."

"Thank your father," the Duchess said.
   "Really he's clever;
   If he hadn't sneezed,
      you'd have been toads forever."

The witch was so angry,
she started to yell,
"I'll never forgive you—
you've broken my spell."
With a terrible shriek, like the voice of doom,
She flew away on her ancient broom.

The family watched as she flew away.
"Well, girls," said the Duchess, "you've had quite a day.
Now let's hurry home, for it's growing quite late
And we've so far to go till we come to our gate."

They all ran so fast they were breathless and hot,
For they wanted no spells again, no, they did not.
They continued to run till they reached their own door;
And they vowed that they'd not wander off any more.

It was Halloween and the trees were bare;
There were ghosts and goblins everywhere.
Up in the castle, secure and cozy,
The little girls frolicked, their faces rosy.
They had apples to bob for and nuts to roast,
And games to be played; but what they liked most
Was joining the Duchess and hearing her tell
How their father had broken that evil spell.
And they always remembered that witch so mean
Who had turned them to toads on Halloween.